SAM PARROW TAKES TIME TO SAVE A DODO

Sam's 4th Exciting Time Travel Adventure

Gill Parkes

ISBN: 9798536707586
Imprint: Independently published

Cover design by: Art Painter
Library of Congress Control Number: 2018675309
Printed in the United States of America

For my favourite animal lovers, Madeleine and Noah, may you always love and care for animals as much as you do now.

And for Matilda, who wanted a story about the commandments. The most important ones are over the page.

Granny xx

"'Love the Lord your God with all your heart and with all your soul and with all your mind.' This is the first and greatest commandment. And the second is like it: 'Love your neighbour as yourself.'"

MATTHEW CH 22 VS 37-39 NIV

CONTENTS

MAP OF ISRAEL

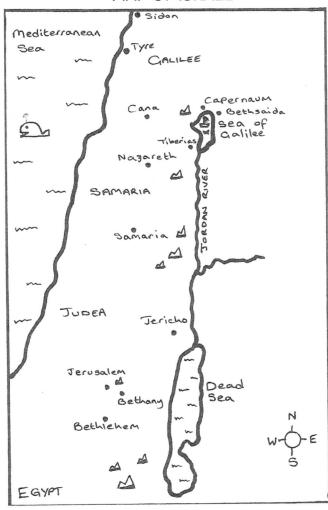

LIST OF CHARACTERS

Alan Taylor – *Missionary*

Andy & Jo – *Sam's parents*

Alex, Ben, Jamie & Kate – *Sam's friends, 21st Century*

Centurion – *Roman commander*

Chris – *Youth group leader*

Eli & Dinah – *Matthew's uncle & aunt*

Jamie's grandparents – *Visitors from Ghana*

Jesus – *Rabbi, miracle worker*

King Uzziah – *King of Babylon*

Liam & Rory – *Youth group friends*

Logan & Dayle - *Kate's brother & sister*

Matthew – *Sam's friend, 1st Century*

Mr Davies – *French teacher*

Mr Stevens – *PE Teacher*

Naamah – *Noah's wife*

Noah – *Ark builder*

Ollie & Jack – *Year 7 bullies*

Rachel – *Sam's friend, 1st Century*

Sam – *12-yr-old time traveller*

Shem, Ham & Japheth (& wives) – *Noah's sons*

CHAPTER 1

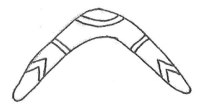

"Je m'appelle Sam. J'ai douze ans et je suis petit. Mes cheveux sont bruns et J'ai les yeux bleus. J'aime nager dans le mer."

"My name is Sam. I am twelve years old and I am small. My hair is brown and my eyes are blue. I like to swim in the sea."

There, that would have to do. Sam put down his pen and rubbed his eyes. Why couldn't everyone speak the same language? His French homework had been to write a few sentences about himself but he didn't know enough to write anymore. He had wanted to write that he loved surfing but he didn't know the word for surf. Sam supposed that it would be useful one day if he ever went to France. Unfortunately, telling people what he looked like when they could see for themselves wasn't going to get him very far!

It was funny how easily he understood every-one when the time stone took him to Israel. There were never any problems with communicating there, except when he forgot and spoke about things like aeroplanes or TV that no one had ever heard of before. He had found the stone while on holiday in Norfolk and since then he had travelled back to the past and seen lots of events that had later been written about in the bible. He had even spoken to Jesus, asking him to visit his friend's aunt and make her well. When they'd gone back to see her the next day she was sweeping the floor and singing, completely healed! Finding the stone had completely changed his life.

He still got bullied occasionally by Ollie and Jack but he was able to brush it off more now that he had real friends to hang around with. When Alex had invited him to the church youth group on Fri-day evenings, Sam had been reluctant to go at first. Then, after his first trip to Bethlehem where he met Rachel, he began to learn about God and the love he had for his people. Strangely, that love also seemed to include Sam and the revelation made him want to find out more. Anyway, he agreed to meet Alex and the result was a bunch of great friends and a cool youth leader who Sam could offload to. Then there was Kate.

Kate was unlike anyone he had ever met before. Energetic, loud, full of life and laughter, red-haired Kate had come to his rescue when Jack had strewn the contents of his rucksack over the path before throwing it over the school fence. For some reason, she had decided to befriend him and had ended up going with him on his last trip to Bethlehem. Normally, Kate was never stuck for something to say but she had been very quiet after they had met Jesus. Back at home in the twenty-first century, Kate had told Sam that Jesus had spoken to her, calling her by name. They realised that not only did he know who they were, he also knew where and when they were from!

Packing away his homework Sam got ready to go out. He had hoped to get most of it done before the weekend but he had spent so much time on his French that he hadn't had time to do anything else. At least his English should be a lot quicker, writing a short story would be easy with all the experiences he'd had in ancient Israel lately!

Arriving at the church hall, Sam saw Jamie

standing outside speaking on his phone. As he got close enough to hear Sam realised that Jamie was speaking French. Amazed at the ease with which he spoke, Sam stood in front of him open-mouthed. Jamie ended the call and greeted Sam,

"Bonsoir!" he said, "Oh, sorry, I mean hi, how're you doing?"

"Hi, I didn't know you spoke French," exclaimed Sam, "Are you French?" he added, frowning.

"Ghanaian, my parents came here when I was small. They speak English and French in Ghana so Dad speaks French to me and Mum speaks English so I get to learn both. That was Dad telling me not to be late home. My grandparents are arriving to-morrow and we have to leave early to pick them up from the airport."

Sam groaned, "I wish I'd known," he said, "I've just spent ages on my French homework. You could have helped!"

Jamie shook his head and laughed as the two boys went inside. A lot of the kids in his class used to ask for help but he had promised his parents that he wouldn't after he had got into trouble for doing someone else's homework. In the end, the teachers' had decided it was a waste of time for him to be there and moved him to Spanish.

Inside the hall, an area had been set aside for a display of pictures and objects from around the world. Sam and his friends wandered over to one of the tables and looked at the things that were on it.

"Isn't that a didgeridoo?" asked Alex.

"Yeah and that's a boomerang," answered Sam, "I wonder what it's all about."

"We've had a missionary staying with us this week," said Ben, "I bet it's something to do with him." He sighed, it had been interesting hearing some of the stories the missionary had told them over dinner but having him stay meant that his Dad had even less time for Ben.

The boys played a round of table football then Sam and Jamie teamed up against Alex and Ben for table tennis. They had just declared a draw when the bell rang for the end of the session. Chris called them to order and the group quietened down.

"Welcome everyone, it's good to see you all again. This week we are honoured to have Mr Alan Taylor with us to tell us about his missionary work with an organisation that works throughout the world, learning the languages and cultures of other people groups. They aim to translate God's word into a language they can understand. We're finishing games early as Alan will be showing a short film before speaking to us during the God Slot."

"Do we get popcorn?" someone asked. The rest of the group laughed while Chris rolled his eyes.

"Not that kind of film, Liam, but while we're on the subject of your stomach," Chris was interrupted by loud laughter and shouts from Liam's friends, "there will be a barbecue on Sunday afternoon in the hall garden. You are all invited to bring your parents, grandparents, brothers and sisters, but please leave your dogs, cats and canaries at home!"

"What about my hamster?" asked Liam, not to be outdone.

"Only if you want him grilled!" answered Rory, his best mate. Chris grinned and held up his hand for quiet.

"Okay, listen up. We've set up a couple of tables with various pictures and objects from around the world. Have a look during break and see if you recognise anything and can say where they're from. Alan will be talking about some of the countries they come from later."

After collecting their snacks the boys inspected the objects on the tables. The didgeridoo and boomerang were obviously from Australia but some of the items on the other table were a mystery.

"So what do you think this is then?" asked Sam, picking up a strange-looking pipe.

"Dunno but what do you think of this?" asked Ben, holding a grass skirt against his jeans.

"Yeah suits you, you should get one for the summer!" grinned Alex. Jamie had gravitated to the drum and started to beat out a rhythm. Before long a small crowd had gathered round to listen. Kate started to stamp her feet and move to the beat, someone else began to clap. The crowd around the tables grew as others joined in, clapping and dancing. Dayle began a song of praise and soon everyone was joining together to give thanks to God. Jamie brought his drumming to a crescendo and finished with a flourish.

"Wow, that was awesome!" Sam grinned at Jamie who was looking well pleased with himself.

"Yeah, I enjoyed that. Grandpa taught me, he used to play in his village festivals."

"Do you get to see them much?" asked Alex.

"Every year – either we go to Ghana or they come here. They're arriving tomorrow so you'll get to meet them on Sunday."

Alan started collecting up some of the more unusual objects for his talk.

"The drum is from Papua New Guinea, it's called a kundu," he said, "Maybe your grandfather would agree to drum with you, you were very good."

Jamie grinned as he handed the drum back to its owner, "Yeah, maybe."

Both the film and Alan's talk were very interesting, Sam hadn't realised there were so many languages in the world, with over eight hundred of them just in Papua New Guinea! He found himself thinking again about the problems of communicating with people around the world. Why on earth did God make it so difficult for everybody? Surely if everyone spoke the same language there would be fewer problems. Sam resolved to ask Rachel the next time he met her although he realised he may have to wait till he met her as a grown-up before he got an answer!

CHAPTER 2

A low hum woke Sam from a deep sleep. He had been dreaming about being in a crowded room where everyone was speaking in a different language. All he had wanted was a glass of water to quench his thirst but he couldn't make anyone understand, it had been incredibly frustrating. Sitting up, he rubbed his eyes and picked up the stone that was on his bedside table. The hum got louder as its strange blue light filled the room. In a flash, Sam was once more sat on a hillside in Bethlehem, shaking his head to clear the dizziness that accompanied time travel. He was dressed just like every other shepherd boy or girl, in tunic and sandals with a rope belt around his middle. Carefully placing the time stone in the pouch attached to his belt, he looked up to see his friend, Rachel, coming towards him. She flopped down onto the grass next to Sam.

"Hello again," she said, "Before you ask, it's the next day!" Sam grinned, he never knew how long he'd been away, sometimes he returned minutes after he had left, other times it was a few days. He had thought at first that it was just random but now it seemed the stone may have a plan. Certainly, everything had seemed to be connected the last time it had brought him to Israel.

"So, did you ask your rabbi about why some people were healed and others weren't?" asked Rachel, referring to the question they had both asked the last time he had seen her.

"Yes, and he spoke about some things being the consequence of our actions."

"What do you mean?"

"Well, if we do something we shouldn't we should expect to see the things that happen because of it." Sam was struggling to explain so that Rachel would understand. He thought of all the things that people did in his own time that caused them harm. Things like eating too much junk food, getting drunk and taking drugs. All those things affected your body, spoiling lives that would otherwise have been good and healthy. He wasn't sure he could explain all that to Rachel though, he didn't know if they did those things in her time. Then he had an idea.

"A bit like the lamb when I first met you," he said, "If he hadn't wandered away from his Ima he wouldn't have got lost and got tangled up in the thorn bush. I'm guessing that if we hadn't found him he would have died."

"Yes of course, but what about King Uzziah? He did say sorry eventually but he never got better."

"No, he didn't. Chris said that his illness was probably to remind him that he would never be as good or as powerful as Yahweh. It stopped him from being proud and helped him to become a better person."

"That's a terrible way to learn a lesson!"

"I know, but I suppose it's better than not learning it at all. Yahweh did forgive him but he wanted Uzziah to remember what he had learned."

"Yes, I suppose he would have forgotten just like the Israelites forgot all the wonderful things Yahweh did for them when they escaped from Egypt."

Sam nodded, we do need to be reminded, he thought, it's so easy to forget about God when everything is great and we think our lives are going well. People always seem to think they don't need him in the good times. They forget that it's

God who gives them everything and it's God who can just as easily take it all away!

In Sam's pouch, the stone began to hum. Taking it out, Sam grinned at Rachel.

"Ready?" he said.

"Ready!" she answered as she grabbed onto his arm.

CHAPTER 3

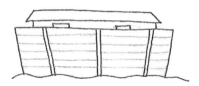

It was pitch black, they couldn't even see their hands in front of them and the effects of travelling through time were made worse by the gentle rocking of wherever they were.

"I feel sick," groaned Rachel as her stomach gave another lurch.

"Me too," said Sam, taking deep breaths to try to get his stomach to settle. Unfortunately, this made him cough as the place they were in was very smelly!

"I wonder where we are?" Rachel felt the floor around her. They were inside somewhere but she had no idea where they could be. Soft snuffles and grunts sounded all around them and a tiny patter of feet was accompanied by the squeaks of mice. Footsteps and muffled voices sounded from above. The children strained to hear what was being said but they were too far away. They clung nervously to each other, afraid of what might happen next. A loud thud startled them as a door banged open, making them jump. Through the open door, a stream of light filtered into the room and they heard someone climb down some steps from the room above. There was enough light for Sam and Rachel to see they were safely hidden behind a large stack of hay bales. The man walked towards them, lighting lamps as he went. Light flooded the space revealing an enormously long, wide room. The children quietly crept forward and looked around. They could see various animals in pens, each pen holding two or more of the same kind. Sam looked at Rachel and grinned.

"We're on Noah's ark!" he whispered excitedly. Rachel hugged herself in delight at the thought of being on the ark that had rescued every type of animal from the Great Flood.

"It must be huge," she whispered, awed by the size of the space they were in. Sam nodded, reluctant to speak in case the man discovered their hiding place. How on earth could they explain themselves being there when everyone else in the world had drowned?

When all the lamps had been lit, the man went

to another door further along the deck. Opening it, he went down more steps to the deck below where he proceeded to light the lamps down there. Sam and Rachel cautiously crept out from their hiding place and looked at the animals that were housed in the pens. Sheep, goats, cows and pigs were housed alongside donkeys, horses and alpacas. As they worked their way along they could see smaller animals like rabbits, cats, guinea pigs and hedgehogs housed in cages large enough to give them room to move around. Rachel was exclaiming over all the animals, asking questions about the many varieties she had never seen before. Hearing a noise back in the direction they had come from Sam looked around for somewhere to hide. A second man had come down the steps and was busily filling the animals feeding troughs from a bucket. Not able to see a suitable hiding place they quietly made their way to the second door and peered down the steps to find out what animals were housed below. A loud trumpeting sound greeted them, causing Rachel to shake with fear.

"Elephants!" declared Sam.

"Ele – what?" asked Rachel who had neither seen nor heard of them before.

"Elephants," repeated Sam, "I love them, they're so huge! We must go down and have a look!" Sam quickly climbed down the steps, forgetting about the need to stay hidden in his excitement at being so close to such huge creatures. Rachel followed more carefully, not at all sure about what she was about to see. This deck was taller than the first so a second set of steps led down from a small platform. When she finally stood in front of the biggest creature she had ever seen in her life, Rachel stood open-mouthed in astonishment. The smaller of the two creatures lowered its head and stretched out its trunk towards her.

"That will be the female, they're always smaller," said Sam. Rachel stood very still as the animal waved her trunk around the girl. "She's smelling you," laughed Sam, "She's probably saying hello!" Rachel reached out to touch the elephant's snaking grey trunk, surprised at how gentle the great creature was.

"She's beautiful," she whispered. A noise from further along the deck caused the children to draw back into the shadows. They found themselves standing next to four long, spindly legs with very knobbly knees. Looking up, Rachel exclaimed when she saw its long neck with its head almost touching the ceiling.

"Whatever is it?" she asked.

"A giraffe, they're the tallest creatures in the world. Both elephants and giraffes live in Africa, a huge continent south of Egypt."

Just then, the giraffe bent its neck so Rachel was face to face with it. She could see the two small horns on the top of its head and when she looked into its large gentle brown eyes with their long eyelashes she fell in love with it immediately.

"Oh, my goodness," she said, "You are gorgeous!"

The two children were so wrapped up in watching the giraffe that they didn't see the man who had lit the lamps come alongside them.

"What's this?" he said, "Stowaways?" Wide-eyed with fear, Rachel and Sam turned to see the man looking at them curiously, "How did you two get on board?"

"Er, I think Yahweh brought us," stammered Sam. Rachel nodded in agreement, unable to speak in fear of what might happen to them.

"Well, you'd best go up top then, down here is for the animals, not for the likes of you. Come on, I suppose you'll want to be fed too!" Leading the way back up the steps, the man closed the door behind him.

"Yahweh has done a good job of keeping them all calm but it's better if we keep the decks separated," he said, "I'll come back to feed them after I've taken you two to see Abba!"

At the top of the third set of steps, they reached the upper deck where Noah was busy filling buckets with grain for his sons to take down to the animals.

"Abba, Yahweh has sent us two more passengers!" Noah looked up in surprise and peered at the two stowaways who stood shivering nervously in front of him.

"Indeed he has my son. Shalom, welcome to our floating kingdom!"

Rachel and Sam looked at each other, surprised that Noah hadn't asked them what they were doing there. Sam at least was thankful as he had no idea how to answer!

"Shalom and thank you for your hospitality," said Rachel, remembering her manners.

Noah smiled, "Shem, perhaps you could ask your Ima for some bread and water for our guests." Noah invited them to sit on a bale of hay while he finished his task. "When you are refreshed you can help Shem feed the animals on the lower deck. There is much work to be done to keep Yahweh's creation healthy!"

"Don't you want to know who we are and how we got here?" asked Sam, puzzled by Noah's apparent acceptance of their presence on the ark.

"All in good time. You could only be here with Yahweh's permission so I have no intention of suggesting that he did not bring you. We will hear your story later when we gather for our meal. In the meantime, the animals must eat before we do!"

CHAPTER 4

Rachel and Sam spent the rest of the morning helping Shem to feed the animals on the lower deck. Sam was kept busy answering Rachel's many questions as she encountered all of the strange and wonderful creatures that she had never seen or heard of before. It pleased Sam that for once, he knew more than Rachel did. The lower deck housed all of the really big creatures like the hippopotamus, rhinoceros, lion and tiger. The children were very wary of the lion and lioness but strangely, the animals were very calm and gentle. They asked Shem why the animals were not behaving like they usually did in the wild.

"Yahweh has brought them here to be cared for so that when the flood goes down they can start over again. He wants all the species to survive so he has made them peaceful just as they used to be when they were first created at the beginning of time. You can see that the only things we are feeding them with are grain, fruit and vegetables, even the meat-eaters like these ate like this at the beginning. Once there are enough of them to survive in their natural habitat they'll go back to being the creatures we know them to be now."

The children thought this was a good answer although they still kept their distance from some of the scarier creatures. Once the feeding had been completed Shem took them back up to the top deck. There they met the rest of the family, Noah's wife Naamah, their other sons, Ham and Japheth and the wives of the three brothers. Naamah took charge of the children and showed them where to wash before they sat down to eat.

"Now, let us thank Yahweh for his provision and protection and we can enjoy the food prepared for us," Noah smiled at his wife who nodded and smiled gratefully. The men and their wives had the task of caring for all the creatures that Yahweh had sent to them but it was her task to feed the family!

Over the meal, Noah asked the children how Yahweh had brought them to the ark. Knowing that this was the furthest back in time they had ever been, Sam wasn't sure how much he should tell. In the end, he just said that he had met Rachel while she was caring for her sheep and Yahweh had picked them up and placed them on the ark.

"But where have you been until now?" asked Naamah, "The rain stopped many months ago and the water is subsiding."

Rachel shrugged and said, "We just know that one minute we were on the hillside and the next we were behind the hay bales near the sheep. It was dark until Shem came down to light the lamps. It was very frightening not knowing where we were."

"Oh my dear, of course you were frightened! We do not doubt you, we are only curious as to why you are here now!" Naamah smiled kindly at the children while the others nodded in agreement.

"Yahweh's ways are his own," declared Noah, "Who are we to question what he does? You are here, therefore he must have great plans for you. That is enough for us, you are welcome!"

Sam breathed a sigh of relief, thankful that he didn't need to say any more. Noah obviously trusted Yahweh and accepted that however strange the children's arrival was if Yahweh had brought them it was for good reason.

As Naahmah began to clear the table, Noah suggested that he take the children on a tour of the ark.

"There are many creatures here that I'm sure you will not have seen before. Come, let me introduce you to Yahweh's wonderful creation!"

Rachel and Sam followed Noah down the steps to the deck below. As they walked from one end of the deck to the other Sam realised that the ark was the biggest floating zoo ever. Rachel was entranced by the many different creatures, most of which she had never heard of. Even Sam struggled with some of them, needing to ask Noah about animals such as pangolins and quolls, as well as quite a few others. They laughed at the platypus, cuddled the koala and were amazed at the many varieties of colourful birds. Representatives of all Yahweh's creatures from the smallest ant to the largest elephant were housed somewhere on the ark.

Some, like the bear and tortoise, were fast asleep in hibernation. Caterpillars had wrapped themselves up in their cocoons ready for the time when the land returned and they could stretch their wings and fly away. Even annoying creatures like wasps and flies had found refuge somewhere on the ark. Not even the tiniest insect that existed at the time of the flood had been missed.

Which was why, when they came to the dodos, Sam just stood in front of them in silence. He realised that despite Noah's efforts to save them these, along with many other animals, no longer existed in his time. Was this why Yahweh had brought them here he wondered? It didn't seem right that Noah had done all this work to save every type of animal on the planet only to have mankind destroy them in the future.

After their tour, Noah took them back up to the top deck where Naamah was waiting to show them where they would sleep. She explained the routine they followed on the ark which was all about caring for the animals. Their needs came first and everyone had a job to do to make sure the animals stayed healthy. Rachel and Sam would be expected to play their part and help out.

Over the next few weeks, the two children joined Noah and his family as they cared for the creatures on the ark. They fed and watered them, cleaned up after them, groomed them and played with them. Well some of them, they still weren't too sure about the lions, or the crocodiles with their rows of sharp teeth.

This was the longest they had been away on a trip with the time stone, so long in fact that Sam's hair had grown and was beginning to look very untidy! Sam wondered if he ought to be concerned, it would be awful if his parents were worried about him, but in all honesty, he was having too much fun! Besides, the stone had always taken him back home to the time he left and he didn't see why this trip should be any different. He did wonder how he was going to explain the length of his hair though!

"I think the giraffes are my favourite," said Rachel, "But I do like to cuddle the rabbits and Koalas."

"And anything else that's small and furry," laughed Sam, thinking about all the other creatures that seemed to end up in Rachel's arms.

"So, they're cute!" she smiled, "Besides, I saw you cuddling a gorilla yesterday!"

"Er, no, she was cuddling me!" laughed Sam.

Being on the ark was hard work but the children were enjoying themselves immensely. They were learning a lot about the different types of animals too. Sam still felt sad when he thought about the dodos though, not that he would say anything to Noah. He didn't think that would be a good idea at all, especially if he knew the reason they were extinct was that their island home had been taken over by humans! They were so gentle and friendly, they weren't afraid of him at all, perhaps that was why they no longer existed.

Eventually, after many weeks of living inside the biggest zoo on the planet, Noah decided it was time to take a look at the world outside.

CHAPTER 5

Noah carried the cage containing the doves up to the top deck. He opened a window and gently taking one of the birds in his hands he set it free. The dove flew around for a while but finding nowhere to land it returned to the ark. Noah placed the dove back in the cage and closed the window. A week of feeding, cleaning up and grooming went by before Noah once again took the doves to the window and set one free. This time the bird stayed out all day, returning in the evening with a freshly plucked leaf from an olive tree!

There was much rejoicing that night as Noah and his family realised that their confinement on the ark was almost at an end. Another week passed however before Noah repeated the experiment. This time the dove did not return and they all knew that Yahweh had dried up the waters and restored life to the land. That evening Rachel,

Sam, Noah and his family, all praised Yahweh for bringing the Great Flood to an end.

"So can we go out now?" asked Sam who was keen to run around on the grass.

"Not just yet," replied Noah, "We must wait for Yahweh's permission. He has entrusted us with a precious task and we do not want to fail him."

Sam nodded, knowing the fate of the dodo and other animals like it, he wasn't so sure he wanted them to leave the ark at all! It would be good to see trees and flowers again though.

"Time for bed I think," declared Naamah, "We still have much work to do before we leave!"

It was almost another two months before Noah heard Yahweh tell him to take everyone out of the ark. During that time the work of caring for the animals carried on as before. No one complained, they all got on with their tasks knowing that they were doing their very best for Yahweh's precious creatures.

Eventually, the day came when Noah opened the huge doors that Yahweh had himself closed the year before. While Noah and his sons released the animals on the lower deck, Rachel and Sam carried the many cages of birds up to the top where the wives were waiting to release them from the window. Some flew off straight away, others fluttered around the ark as though unsure of their new-found freedom. Eventually, all the cages but two were empty and the trees were once more filled with song as birds flew back and forth to build their nests.

With the lower deck empty, the men turned their attention to the middle one. Animals of all types were guided down the ramps and set free. Sam and Rachel had gone down to help with the cages of smaller animals and Sam noticed that the sheep and cows were being held back.

"Why aren't they being let out?" he asked.

"For the same reason that some of the doves and pigeons are still in their cages," replied Rachel, "Once the ark is empty Noah will build an altar and sacrifice one of each kind as a thank offering to Yahweh."

Sam looked horrified, "But we've been caring for them for months!"

"And Yahweh has been caring for all of us. It is only right that we show him how grateful we are."

31

Sam thought sadly of the creatures he had come to love. He had wondered why there seemed to be more of some kinds. Now he knew.

"Come on, help me carry these hives outside," Rachel said to Sam in an attempt to distract him from the fate of the sheep. Sam sighed, he was beginning to understand the meaning of sacrifice, realising that it was only worthwhile if you gave up something you loved or valued. Anything less would be meaningless.

Collecting a hive from the shelf, Sam followed Rachel down the ramp. These bees were essential to pollinate the plants so that there would be food for everyone in the future. They carefully placed the hives amongst the trees. As the sun gently warmed them the hives were filled with the sound of humming as the bees began to wake. It reminded Sam of his time stone which was still safely stored in his pouch. He wondered if it may soon be time for them to be leaving too.

With the ark finally empty, Noah found some large rocks and built an altar. Sam and Rachel had gathered dry leaves and sticks from around the trees so that they could build a fire. They watched as Noah slaughtered the animals chosen for sacrifice and placed them on the altar. The sweet smell as they cooked on the fire filled the air, making Sam think of home. He remembered the barbecue that was planned at church all those weeks ago. Had he missed it? Were people worried about where he was? Or would he go back to the same night that the time stone had woken him from sleep?

A rumble of thunder sounded above. Sam looked up expecting to see dark rain clouds but the sun shone brightly and there were just a few fluffy white clouds scudding across the beautiful blue sky. It was good to be outside again after all those weeks on the ark. Suddenly, the clearest and most beautiful rainbow appeared and everyone gasped in wonder at the purity of its colours. It may not have been the first they had ever seen but it was by far the best.

"This is a sign of my promise to you," a loud voice rang out across the land, "Never again will floods fill the earth and destroy all life that is on it. Whenever I see my bow in the clouds I will remember my promise to you and all the living creatures that live on the earth."

As Noah, his three sons and each of their wives worshipped Yahweh, none of them noticed that

Rachel and Sam were no longer with them.

CHAPTER 6

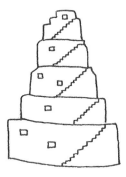

The children were standing in a bustling town square. The people around them were busy buying and selling at the market or standing in small groups chatting to one another. Businessmen stood on the steps of the town hall having heated discussions while children raced around laughing and calling to one another. Wherever it was the stone had brought them to was very loud with the sounds of people talking. Rachel and Sam felt a little overwhelmed by the noise after the peace of the world they had just left. They wandered about the square, listening to what people said in an attempt to find out where they were. A delegation of important looking people came down the steps towards the place where Rachel and Sam were standing. As they walked past, Sam heard one of them say something about going to the tower.

"Let's follow them," he said, grabbing Rachel's hand to pull her along in the same direction.

"Yes but not too close! They may be going to somewhere we're not allowed."

They followed the group past all the market stalls and out through the town gate. Carrying on a little way down the road they came to a river and the children could see it was a hive of activity. Next to the river, a group of workmen were moulding clay into bricks which were then left to dry in the sun. These were then collected by another group who baked the bricks in a large oven. Two boys took turns feeding sticks onto the fire beneath. It was far too hot for either of them to stay close for too long. A second oven, its fire now out, was being emptied of the cooled bricks inside it. Once emptied, the fire would be re-lit, the oven filled with bricks of sun-baked clay and the hardening process started all over again.

"I wonder what all those bricks are for?" asked Rachel.

"There are certainly a lot of them, maybe they are extending the town."

They continued to watch as the cooled bricks were carefully stacked onto a cart that had a donkey strapped to the shafts at the front. The group they were following stopped to inspect the bricks, each picking one up and turning it over, looking for cracks and flaws. The most important looking one, who seemed to be the leader, nodded at the others and smiled.

"Excellent quality," he said, "They are exactly what is needed for our growing city."

The group replaced the bricks and turned back towards the town but instead of returning through the gate, they followed a path to the right. As they rounded the corner, the children could see a tall tower was being built. The tower was round with steps spiralling up the outside and a group of workmen stood on a platform at the top of a tall scaffold, placing another layer of bricks onto the wall. They were kept well supplied with bricks by a team of men going up and down the steps.

"Wow, they're well organised," said Sam, "That tower will be finished in no time!" Sam was impressed by the efficiency of the workforce, especially as they didn't have all the advantages of the twenty-first century.

"Yes, but I think Yahweh will have something to

say about all that," said Rachel as she suddenly had an idea about where they could be.

"Why, do you know where we are then?" asked Sam.

"Babel I think. The people wanted to build a huge city with a tower that reached up to the heavens."

"Ah, I'm guessing Yahweh wasn't too keen on that idea."

"No, he wasn't. He actually came to have a look at what they were doing. Maybe we'll see him!"

Sam gulped, see Yahweh? Seriously? The last time he saw him he was hidden in a cloud that flashed with lightning! Admittedly he sounded friendly enough when he gave Noah the covenant with the rainbow but that didn't mean Sam wanted to be around when he turned up this time.

"Do we know what he looks like?" asked Sam.

"Not really. We are told in the Torah that when he first walked in the garden with Adam he looked just like a man but that was because he wanted Adam to get to know him. I suppose the best way to do that was to spend time together and it was probably easier for Adam if Yahweh looked like he did."

"So how will we know if it's him?"

"I don't know, we'll just have to watch and see what happens."

While they were talking the men at the top of the tower started to dismantle the scaffold. It appeared that the tower was finished! The group of men they had followed stood at the bottom admiring the building and exclaiming over their achievement. They sounded very proud of themselves and they discussed all the great things they were going to do. A crowd of people began to gather at the bottom.

On the opposite side of the tower to where Sam and Rachel were standing, three men stood looking intently at the group. Sam had a strange feeling that he knew them.

"Er, Rachel, who are they over there?"

Rachel turned to where Sam was looking and a small shiver ran down her spine.

"I think that's Yahweh."

"Who's with him?"

"I'm not sure, angels maybe? They seem to be discussing something. Maybe they're deciding what to do about the tower."

As they watched, the tallest of the three raised his head and spoke but the children were too far away to hear what he said. A gentle breeze began to blow from their direction, ruffling the hair of everyone it touched. No one was missed out, not even Sam and Rachel. Strange sounds and words could be heard as the people continued with their conversations. Every so often someone would shake their head and stop, then try again more loudly in an effort to be understood. Some of them looked frightened, everyone was confused. They began to separate as each person looked for someone they could understand and who could understand them. The tallest tower in the world was abandoned as the people desperately sought others who spoke in a language the same as theirs.

On the other side of the wall, in the town, the cries of children got louder as they raced back to their mothers. All their play and laughter had stopped.

Rachel turned to Sam and grinned, she spoke to him to tell him what was happening but her words sounded strange and Sam didn't understand her.

"I don't know what you said. I can't understand you," he said shaking his head, a look of panic in his eyes. Sam remembered his dream the night that the stone woke him and took him to meet Rachel. His feelings of frustration at not being understood were nothing compared with how he felt now. Rachel frowned, her stomach sinking as she tried desperately to understand what Sam had said but no matter how hard they tried they couldn't make themselves understood. The children looked at each other in horror as they realised that whatever had happened to the people of Babel had happened to them too.

CHAPTER 7

Thankfully they hadn't had to wait long before the time stone whisked them back to Bethlehem. Sitting on the grass, everything looked to be just how it was when they had left all those months ago before spending time on the ark.

"I think we're back to the time we left," said Sam tentatively, glancing at Rachel and willing her to understand him.

"Yes, I believe we are!" grinned Rachel. They laughed in relief as their distress at not being able to communicate with each other fell away.

"Wow, that was scary!" said Sam.

"I know, I hated that we couldn't understand each other."

"No wonder the city was abandoned. They weren't able to tell each other what to do."

"Yes, I think that was Yahweh's intention. He

didn't want them to achieve such great things that they forgot about him."

"We have though. In my time we have learned each other's languages and done a lot of things that people used to think were impossible."

"People communicate better here too. Maybe they just weren't ready then. That time wasn't so long after the flood, even Noah's sons were still alive. I think Noah may have been too although he was very old."

"How old was he when he died?"

"950 years old!"

"Wow, that's ancient! Nobody lives that long now!"

"No, they don't here either. I suppose people still needed to live for a long time after the flood so that they could have lots of children. Don't forget, they were the only people on the earth for ages. They didn't live as long as Noah though and it got less and less as time went on."

"I'm glad, I don't think I'd want to live that long."

"Me neither," agreed Rachel, "I'm glad we went to the ark though, it was fun."

"Yes, it was. I didn't mind that it was hard work, I just enjoyed being with all the different animals."

"There were so many. I didn't realise the world

was so big!"

Sam smiled, they had both learnt a lot about God's world while they were on the ark and at Babel, he had learnt why he struggled with his French homework!

"I think I should go back to my brothers," said Rachel, "Just to make sure they haven't been worried about me."

"I'll see you when I come back then, I wonder where the stone will take us next time?"

"No idea, just make sure you do come back!" laughed Rachel as she ran down the slope to the camp. Sam looked at the stone which had started to hum as soon as Rachel left.

"It must be God doing this," he thought, "How else would the stone always work at exactly the right time?" And with a flash of blue light, Sam was back in his bed in the twenty-first century.

He checked the time and date on the clock sitting on his bedside table, it was the same time and date when he had left to meet Rachel before being taken to the ark. Snuggling under his duvet, Sam sighed with relief. It would have been awful if his parents had thought he'd gone missing and how on earth would he explain now that he had come home? Yawning quietly, Sam turned over and went to sleep.

Standing in the shower the next morning Sam was very grateful that he lived in the twenty-first century. This was a definite improvement to the buckets of cold water they'd washed in on the ark! As he rinsed the soap out of his hair he began to laugh, four months of hair growth had disappeared in a flash and he was back to his normal self. Well, almost, he may look the same but he certainly didn't feel the same anymore. Sam realised that he was beginning to feel a lot more confident about himself and his place in God's world.

He spent the rest of the day working on his homework and enjoying being back in his own home. He had loved being on the ark but the visit to Babel had unsettled him. Also, he had missed his parents, however much they annoyed him at times!

Unfortunately, the experience at Babel hadn't improved his language skills so Sam decided that his French homework was as good as it was going to get. On the other hand, his English was the easiest ever. His short story, "Life on the Ark" was the best thing he'd ever written. Just as he placed the final full stop his dad walked into the room.

"Not going out today Sam?" asked Andy.

"No, I need to finish my homework."

Andy raised his eyebrows, this was not like his son at all!

"Is everything okay?" he asked.

"Sure, it's just, well, there's a barbecue at church tomorrow and I'd like to go. You're invited too," Sam added, looking hopefully at his dad.

"Oh, right. Well, I'll check with your mum but I guess we could come. It would be good to meet your friends." He glanced over Sam's shoulder at the work on the table, "That looks interesting, may I read what you've written?"

Sam handed over his essay and watched Andy's eyes grow wide as he read "Life on the Ark."

"That's excellent!" he said when he got to the end, "It's almost as though you were there. You're right though, it is a shame about the dodos."

Sam grinned, if only he knew!

CHAPTER 8

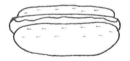

Sunday was warm and dry, a perfect day for a barbecue. Sam's mouth started to water as the smell of sausages sizzling on the hot coals wafted over the garden. He could see Alex and Ben kicking a ball around with Liam and his mates while most of the grown-ups stood around chatting. Everyone seemed to know each other which made Sam feel a little left out. He didn't think he could abandon his parents to join the game but he didn't know who to leave them with.

"Sam, over here!" Kate called out from behind the table that was set out with drinks of various kinds. Sam grinned, just the person he needed to see, he couldn't wait to tell her about his latest adventure! Kate introduced her parents to Sam's, making Sam feel free to drag Kate over to an empty bench near the footie.

"You'll never guess where I've been!" he said, grinning at Kate.

"Oh where, tell me," Kate waited in anticipation.

"The ark, for four whole months!"

"What? How did that happen?"

"I met Rachel in Bethlehem like always and the stone took us to the ark. We had no idea where we were at first as it was so dark and we felt more sick than usual because it was rocking!"

"But you've never stayed anywhere that long before, have you?"

"No, but it was great fun looking after the animals and Noah just accepted that God had put us there for a reason so he didn't ask too many questions."

"Didn't you worry you'd be missed at home?"

"A bit, but I reckoned that the stone always brought us back to the time we left so it would be alright. I was more worried about the state of my hair!"

"Your hair? Why?"

"Because it grew and there was no way to cut it. I don't know how I would have explained that! It was okay though because everything went back to how it was before I left."

Kate's laughter at the thought of Sam with long hair reached Ben just as he was about to score. Missing the space between the two hoodies that acted as a goal he turned round to see who had distracted him. When he realised that it was Sam and Kate and he saw how well they were getting on, Ben frowned. Sam knew that Ben liked Kate, he thought, how dare he sit there making her laugh when Ben got tongue-tied just looking at her! Ben lashed out at the ball, sending it flying over the fence into the neighbour's garden.

"Ben, what are you doing? We'll never get it back now!" Alex said crossly, "What's got into you?"

Ben shrugged, "Sorry," he muttered, knowing that he'd spoilt the game. "I'll go get it, Dad's friends with them, they won't mind." He walked off, hands in his pockets, kicking the grass as he went. Alex wandered over to Sam and Kate while the rest of the players went to find out if the food was ready.

"I don't know what's got into him, he was fine a minute ago!" grumbled Alex.

"Maybe he was cross because he missed," suggested Kate.

"He's not usually that bothered. He hardly ever gets them in any way!" Alex shook his head and looked at the two friends sat beside each other, "So, what's so funny?"

"Oh, er, not much," blushed Sam, "Just something I'd said that sparked Kate off, you know what she's like!"

"Yeah," agreed Kate, "It doesn't take much, I'll laugh at anything!"

Sam and Kate desperately tried to think of something to say that would stop Alex from asking more questions when Chris announced that food was ready.

As they queued to get their burgers and hot dogs Ben came back with the ball but rather than joining them in the queue, he went to the back of the line. Alex raised his eyebrows at him but Ben ignored him and turned to talk to Jamie who had just arrived with his grandparents. Ben knew that he was being unreasonable but he couldn't help himself. The plain fact was, he was jealous.

Sam covered his hot dog in ketchup and looked around for his parents. He spotted them talking to Chris and a small group of others standing by the drinks table. He sighed with relief, they seemed to be getting on okay so he went over to where Jamie was helping his grandparents find somewhere to sit. Having got them settled he turned his attention to Sam.

"Hey, Sam, enjoying yourself?" he asked.

"Yes, thanks. Not so sure about Ben though. Did he say anything to you?" Sam replied between mouthfuls of bread and sausage. Before Jamie could answer, his grandmother called out to him.

"Gyasi, come, let us meet your friend!"

Jamie grinned and introduced Sam.

"Ete-sen Samuel, are your Agya and Ena here today?"

Sam looked at Jamie for help but he had turned and said something incomprehensible to his grandmother, who laughed.

"Forgive me, Sam, it is my little game! In my language, it is always polite to ask about our families! 'Agya' and 'Ena' are your Father and Mother and 'ete-sen' means 'hello'."

Sam grinned back, he was getting used to this!

"Ete-sen," he replied, "Agya and Ena are over there talking to Chris. What language do you speak?"

Jamie's grandmother looked pleased with Sam's reply.

"We speak Akan which is the language of our people and English which is the language of our country. There are also many people in Ghana who speak French so we speak that too."

Sam was impressed, he wished he could speak three languages! "What did you call Jamie when I came over?" he asked.

"Gyasi, it is his Akan name. It means wonderful child. It is the name we gave to him when he was born because he was such a beautiful baby!"

Jamie rolled his eyes and mouthed an apology to Sam. Fortunately, his parents came over just then so he was saved from any further embarrassment.

The two boys wandered away, looking for their friends.

"Why is Ben ignoring me?" asked Sam.

"Dunno, is he?"

"It was when I was talking to Kate. We were laughing and he glared at me then refused to speak."

"Oh. You two do seem to be getting on rather well. You haven't forgotten how much he likes her have you?"

"What? You think he's jealous?" exclaimed Sam, "There's no need, she's just a friend!"

"Maybe, but it probably doesn't seem like that to Ben!"

Sam groaned, this was getting to be so complicated! He didn't want Ben to be upset but how could he explain about Kate? It wasn't his fault that the stone had taken her with him to first-century Bethlehem!

Back at home, Sam's parents said how much they'd enjoyed the barbecue.

"It was good to meet your friends, Sam," said Andy as he put the kettle on, "Tea, Jo?"

"Yes, please. Chris seemed to be a very sensible young man. He had some interesting things to say about God too," Jo added thoughtfully.

"Mmm, he certainly gave me something to think about."

Sam smiled, "Yeah, they're good mates." He was glad his parents approved, especially of Chris who had helped a lot with the questions Sam asked after his travels through time. Maybe they'd even agree to go to church sometime!

CHAPTER 9

Later that week Sam's French teacher asked him to stay behind after class. Sam groaned, he'd hoped he'd done enough for his homework but it seemed he hadn't.

"It's okay, I won't bite," smiled Mr Davies, "I'm just wondering how we can improve your language skills."

Sam pulled a face, "I don't think I've got any," he said, "Languages aren't really my thing."

"Maybe not but they are important. Sometimes the best way to learn is to be immersed in the language, after all, that is how you learnt English!"

"You mean extra classes?" Sam was horrified, two hours every week at school was bad enough!

Mr Davies laughed, "Don't look so worried, I run a French club after school on Wednesdays. We play games, have quizzes, we even cook sometimes! It's fun, the only rule is that English is not allowed, you may only speak French."

Sam thought about what his teacher had said about being immersed in a language. Maybe that was why Jamie was so good, if his dad only spoke French to him he would have learnt it easily. He'd have had to, otherwise, he'd never be able to talk to him!

"Okay, maybe I'll give it a go," Sam agreed, after all, he had wished he was better at languages when he'd been talking to Jamie's grandmother.

"Excellent, I look forward to you joining us next week. Au revoir, Sam"

"Er, au revoir Monsieur Davies," grinned Sam as he left the room. "Phew," he thought, "That was better than I was expecting. Maybe French club won't be too bad and at least I got an 'A' for English!"

Feeling pleased with himself, Sam ran across the yard to the gate. In his haste to leave school, he didn't see Jack who was coming round the corner from the direction of the sports field. Sam bumped into him, causing Jack to lose his balance and fall to the ground.

"Watch it, Sparrow, you'll regret that!"

"Sorry, it was an accident, I didn't mean it."

"Course you didn't," sneered Jack, trying to get up off the floor, "Ow!" Jack collapsed again and sprawled on the ground looking helpless.

"What's wrong?" asked Sam, concerned for him even though he was his arch-enemy.

"Nothing, just leave me alone," muttered Jack.

"No, you're hurt, let me help." Sam reached out to help Jack stand up but he pushed him away.

"I don't need your help!"

But no matter how hard he tried, Jack couldn't put weight on his left foot without a searing pain bringing tears to his eyes.

Sam shook his head, "I'm going for help," he said as he ran back to the school office.

Eventually, after being helped back into school by one of the teachers, Jack was collected by his Mum who drove him to the local hospital. Sam walked slowly home wondering if he'd be to blame for ending Jack's promising career as an athlete. As it turned out, Sam wasn't to blame at all.

That afternoon, Jack and Ollie had been fooling around on the cricket field and not paying attention to the game. Jack had got in the way of a superb hit by the opposing team captain, the hard ball landing squarely on his left foot. At the time he had laughed it off but his collision with Sam and the resulting fall highlighted his injury.

The next day, Jack came to school on crutches with his broken foot in a cast. The story of how insignificant little Sparrow bested one of the year seven bullies was all around the school.

"Is it true?" asked Alex and Kate when the three met up at break.

"No!" declared Sam, "I just bumped into him that's all. He'd already broken his foot at cricket, it got worse when he fell over."

Sam felt miserable, he'd been worried that he was going to get into trouble but thankfully Jack's mum had rung his and explained what had happened. She was really nice and apologised for Jack's behaviour. Apparently, she'd heard some of the things he'd been doing and although she didn't want to believe them, Jack's attitude towards Sam had changed her mind. He had lied about the accident, saying it was deliberate and hadn't said anything about the incident at cricket. Unfortunately for Jack, Mr Stevens, the PE teacher, had rung her to see how Jack was and told her the truth. Needless to say, Jack was not in her good books. Now everyone was looking at Sam like he was some sort of superhero and he cringed with embarrassment.

Alex grinned, "It's still a good story!" he said.

"Maybe he'll leave you alone now," laughed Kate, "Sam Parrow, Superkid!"

"Ha-ha, don't you start. I think I preferred it when nobody took any notice of what was going on."

"Oh, everyone noticed," replied Kate, "They just didn't want to get involved in case they got bullied too."

"You did though," said Sam, thinking of the time she had helped pick up his stuff after Jack had emptied his school bag and tossed it over the fence. That was when he had shown her the time stone and they'd ended up in Bethlehem. Just then, Ollie sidled over and whispered in Sam's ear.

"You've not heard the last of this, Sparrow!"

Sam sighed, it was one thing putting Jack out of action but it was Ollie who instigated everything and he was still at large.

CHAPTER 10

Heading out of school at the end of the day, Sam found Alex and Kate waiting for him at the gate.

"What are you two doing, playing bodyguard?" asked Sam.

"Something like that. It was Kate's idea."

Kate grinned and raised her arm in salute, "We are charged with guarding the mighty Sparrow, slayer of evil and defender of mankind!"

The two boys rolled their eyes, what was it with girls? Mind you, Kate wasn't exactly like other girls they knew so maybe it was just her!

The three friends walked as far as the turn for Sam's house.

"See you later?" asked Alex, before he carried on

towards his own home. He hesitated, not sure if he should wait for Kate who lived in the same direction. Sam had told him about Ben and assured Alex that there was nothing to worry about but he wasn't so sure. Maybe it was just that she had helped him when no one else had but they did seem a lot friendlier than they used to be.

"Yeah, see you, we need a re-match at table tennis!"

Now it was Kate's turn to roll her eyes, these boys were so competitive!

"You carry on, I'll catch up," she said seeing Alex hesitate, but she wanted to get Sam alone to ask him some more about the ark.

"Okay," Alex nodded and feeling embarrassed he turned for home.

Sam groaned, this was becoming so awkward.

"Sorry," said Kate, "I know what Ben's thinking, but I'm not interested, not in that way. Not with you either!"

"That's a relief, I like being just friends, it's less complicated. I just don't know how to make Ben believe me."

"I'll speak to him tonight. Don't worry, I'll be nice!" she added when she saw Sam's expression.

"Maybe we should get together when the others

aren't around, I have so much to tell you!"

"That would be good, could you come to mine tomorrow?"

Sam agreed and Kate raced off to catch up with Alex.

That evening at youth group, Kate told Ben that nothing was going on between her and Sam and that he was an idiot for thinking there might be. She also told him there wouldn't be anything going on with anyone else either, Ben included.

"And that was supposed to be nice?" asked Sam during break.

Kate shrugged, "I didn't want him getting ideas," she said. Thankfully, Ben had taken it well and relationships settled back to normal. Kate and Sam were careful not to spend too much time together though in case anyone else got the wrong end of the stick.

The next day, Sam made sure his homework was mostly done before going over to Kate's in the afternoon. She had said it was the best time as Dayle and Logan would both be out.

"I don't want them getting the wrong idea either!" she had said when she gave him her address.

Now they were sat under the apple tree in the back garden, drinking homemade lemonade.

"This is much better than the shop stuff," said Sam appreciatively.

"Mum makes it, it's good, isn't it? So, tell me everything!"

Sam grinned and told Kate about his time on the ark and how he'd felt about the dodos. Kate agreed that it was sad but people were becoming much more aware of the need to care for the planet now.

"And the rainbow was awesome, much bigger and clearer than any I've seen before! Then while they were all busy worshipping God, the stone took us to Babel!"

"The place where God mixed up the languages?"

"Yes and he mixed up ours too! It was well scary!"

"So what happened, could you and Rachel understand each other?"

"Not until we got back to Bethlehem. It was such a relief when we could talk to each other again. I think God was showing us what it was like for the people at Babel. It's no wonder they scattered all over the world, they probably didn't trust anyone they couldn't speak to."

The two friends lay back and watched the clouds scudding across the sky. They were talking about what they'd be doing in the summer holidays when Sam noticed a soft hum coming from his pocket. Taking out the time stone he looked at Kate who was grinning like a Cheshire cat.

"Next stop, Bethlehem!" he said as the scenery changed and the apple tree transformed itself into the fig tree in Rachel's garden.

CHAPTER 11

Sam and Kate had just recovered from the dizziness that accompanied time travel when Matthew opened the gate and entered the garden from the street.

"Hello again!" he said when he saw them sitting under the tree, "Have you just come back?"

"Yes, we've been home for almost two weeks," Sam stood up and adjusted the belt around his tunic.

Matthew laughed, "I've just come from Uncle Eli's, Ima is still there talking to Aunt Dinah. I guessed you'd gone home when I came back out and saw that you had both gone."

"You mean it's still the same day that we left?" asked Kate.

Matthew nodded, "Ima is still telling Aunt

Dinah about everything that has happened while she was ill. She won't be back for a while!" Sam and Kate laughed, Rachel was no different to their mothers when they got together with people they hadn't seen for a long time.

"I used to get confused at first," said Sam, "Now I just accept that it is whatever day they say it is!" Kate agreed that travelling through time was decidedly weird, especially when you had no clue as to when or where you were. Right on cue, the time stone began to hum. Holding tightly to one another, the three friends closed their eyes in readiness for their next adventure.

"Pooh!" said Kate, wrinkling her nose at the strong smell of fish.

"Capernaum!" grinned both boys at the same time.

"Now I know what you meant the last time when you said we couldn't be in Galilee. This place stinks, how on earth can people live here?"

"I guess you get used to it. Every place smells of something, you just don't notice it when you're there all the time. I really noticed the smell of traffic when I got back from the ark."

"Oh, Ima told me about that when I was little, I used to love hearing about the different animals," said Matthew, "I didn't understand that she'd actually been there though till I was older."

"I bet the ark was smelly!" Kate screwed up her nose at the thought of all those animals in an enclosed space.

"It was, especially when it was time to clean out their stalls!"

Matthew was curious about why the traffic in Sam's time should smell any different to the traffic in his. Surely it was all the same? Maybe there was just more of it, but more donkeys pulling carts wouldn't smell any different to the ark! He shrugged, Ima wouldn't tell Daniel about the future when they went back in time to Babylon so he supposed that Sam wouldn't tell him either. It was probably just as well, there was enough to think about just hopping through time in and around Israel!

As they wandered down the main street they saw a small crowd of people in front of them. Guessing that Jesus would be in the middle of it they walked over to join them. As they got close, a group of elders hurried up to him and got his attention.

"Master please come with us," they said, "We have been sent by the centurion who built our synagogue. His servant is sick and he has asked that you heal him. Though the centurion is not a Jew he loves our nation and deserves your help."

Jesus agreed and accompanied the elders to the centurion's home. Matthew, Sam and Kate followed in the group close behind. They had no intention of missing what would happen next! They had almost reached the house when some men came out to speak to Jesus.

"We have been sent with this message," they said, "The centurion says, 'Lord, don't trouble yourself, for I do not deserve to have you come under my roof. Just say the word, and my servant will be healed. For I myself am a man under authority, with soldiers under me. I tell this one, 'Go,' and he goes; and that one, 'Come,' and he comes. I say to my servant, 'Do this,' and he does it.' Those were the words he told us to say to you."

When the men had finished speaking, Jesus turned to all those who had followed him. He was amazed at the faith shown by the centurion and he said to the crowd,

"I tell you the truth, I have not found such great

faith even in Israel." Then he told the men to return to the house where they would find the servant restored to health.

Jesus and his followers moved on but Sam held back, wanting to know what Jesus meant.

"The centurion is a Gentile and so he is not expected to believe in Yahweh as we do. Some Gentiles do believe but they don't find it easy to follow our laws and many give up because it's so different to how they were brought up." Matthew paused to think about how best to explain to Sam.

"The centurion expects people to obey him," joined in Kate, "Which means he is a man with authority."

"That's right and he believes that Jesus has the same authority," agreed Matthew.

"So whatever Jesus says goes," said Sam, nodding as he began to see why Jesus was so amazed. Not only did the centurion believe that Jesus could heal his servant he believed that he could do it without even being there. All he needed to do was say the word and it was done!

Just then one of the men that had spoken to Jesus came back out. When he saw the children he smiled and walked over to them.

"Did you see where the Rabbi went?" he asked.

"Down the street, that way, but we didn't see where he went after that," answered Matthew. The man looked disappointed.

"How is the servant?" asked Kate.

"He is well and has gone back to his duties!" replied the man, "I wanted to say thank you, my friend values his servant and would have been upset if he had lost him."

"Well, I'm sure Jesus knows," smiled Kate, "But if we see him we will tell him."

"Thank you, may your god bless you today!" The man smiled and went back into the house.

Left alone in the street the three friends realised that the time stone was humming and in a flash of blue light they were taken to another place at another time.

"Err?" Kate looked questioningly at Sam and Matthew. The boys looked at each other then back at Kate. Matthew shrugged.

"No idea," he said.

Sam shook his head, "Me neither."

"Well, wherever we are it certainly smells better!" Kate looked around the small square and saw a group of people sitting in the shade of a large tree. "Let's go over there and join them," she said.

As they approached, a man stood up and addressed Jesus who was sat with his back to the tree facing the group.

"Rabbi," he asked, "what must I do to inherit eternal life?"

"What is written in the Law?" Jesus replied, "How do you understand it?"

The man considered his answer carefully before saying we should love Yahweh with our whole being and love our neighbour the same way we love ourselves.

"You have answered correctly." Jesus replied, "Do this and you will live."

Again the man considered Jesus' words.

"And who is my neighbour?" he asked.

The three children looked at each other and grinned.

"Storytime!" said Kate. She knew that Jesus loved to teach the people by telling parables to help them understand. Although this would be the first time Matthew heard it, the one Jesus was about to tell now was taught in every Sunday school class in England in the twenty-first century and probably in every other country too!

"A man was going from Jerusalem to Jericho when he was attacked by thieves. They stole his clothes, beat him and left him to die. A priest was travelling the same road but when he saw the man he crossed to the other side. When a Levite came by he also ignored the man and crossed over. Later a Samaritan came along with his donkey but when he saw the man lying in the road he felt sorry for him and helped him. He bandaged his wounds, placed him on the donkey and took him to an inn where he took care of him overnight. The next day he paid the innkeeper to look after the man saying that he would pay any extra that may be needed when he returned."

Jesus looked at the one who had questioned him and asked,

"Which of these three do you think was a neighbour to the man who fell into the hands of thieves?"

"The one who had mercy on him," he replied. Jesus nodded and told him to do the same.

Many of those sitting under the tree looked shocked when Jesus chose a Samaritan as the one to offer help, even Matthew.

Sam turned to his friends and asked, "What was the point of saying they were a priest, a Levite and a Samaritan?"

"I suppose everyone would expect the priest to be the first to help someone in trouble," answered Kate.

"Yes, but he would be worried that he would be made unclean or attacked himself, the same with the Levite," Matthew pointed out.

"What do you mean, unclean?" asked Sam.

"Our law states that if anyone touches someone who is injured or sick they have to wash and spend time away from everyone before they can go back to their duties. That is especially important for the priest, he was probably going to worship at the temple and didn't want to miss it."

"But you can't just leave someone to die!" exclaimed Sam. Kate rolled her eyes.

"It's just a story," she said, "Jesus was using them as examples. The important one is the Samaritan!"

"Why?"

"Because he's a foreigner and a lot of Jews don't like them," sighed Matthew. The truth was that many Jews hated the Samaritans and wouldn't have anything to do with them. The fact that Jesus had spoken of the Samaritan as the one to help instead of one of those who ignored the injured man was something that Matthew was struggling to accept. Deep down he knew that Jesus was right but that didn't make it any easier. Jesus' parable had left him feeling quite uncomfortable as he realised that Jesus was saying that we should help everyone in need, not just the people we liked.

Fortunately for Matthew, the time stone chose that moment to whisk them back to Bethlehem where they heard Rachel fumbling with the gate. Relieved to be home Matthew went to help her and as he did so, the stone flashed once more, taking Sam and Kate back to where they had been lying under the apple tree in Kate's back garden.

CHAPTER 12

Things had settled down at school with everyone getting caught up with end of term activities. Sam suffered the occasional grinning salute from those with nothing better to think about but most people were fully occupied with the approaching sports day and annual Summer Fête. With exams finished, school felt a lot more relaxed and the current heatwave had everyone looking forward to the holidays.

French club wasn't as bad as Sam was expecting although this being his first week he didn't say very much. He was tempted to just sit on the sidelines but the older kids with a good understanding of French made a point of speaking to those who, like Sam, hadn't got a clue. He was surprised to see Jack there but Sam made sure he kept well out of his way so that there wouldn't be any trouble. Hopefully, Jack didn't know enough French to insult him and even if he did, Sam couldn't understand so it wouldn't matter.

Walking home after club, Sam thought about the story that Jesus told about the Samaritan. He'd noticed how uncomfortable Matthew had been so it had obviously hit home with him. Sam hadn't realised until then how badly the Jews and Samaritans felt about each other. He supposed it was a bit like himself and Jack, except Sam didn't hate him, just the stuff he said and did. What was it that man said about the law? It was something like love Yahweh with your whole self and love your neighbour like yourself. That was it and then Jesus told the story to show who our neighbour was, which was basically everybody! So Matthew had to love the Samaritans and he had to love Ollie and Jack. Tall order thought Sam, he reckoned he needed some help from Chris again!

Thankfully, things had settled down with Ben so Friday night saw them resume their weekly round of friendly matches around the various game tables. During break, Sam sought out Chris.

"Hey, Sam, how are you doing? It was good to meet your parents on Sunday."

"I'm good thanks. Yeah, Mum and Dad enjoyed the barbecue, they said you were very interesting!" Sam and Chris both laughed.

"So, what can I do for you, more questions?"

Sam grinned, "Well, you did say I could ask!"

"Indeed and it will be a pleasure to talk with you. So what is it this time?"

Sam explained that he had heard the story of the Samaritan and got that he had to love his enemies but he didn't know how to, or even if he could. Chris agreed that it wasn't easy. He knew about Sam's problem with being bullied as his friends had been concerned and asked Chris for help. Knowing that he couldn't interfere without Sam's permission, he had been praying about it, asking God for wisdom. It seemed like God had answered!

"You're right, it isn't easy. Nothing is on our own, that's why Jesus promised to send his Holy Spirit to help us."

Sam looked puzzled, "How?" he asked.

"When we trust Jesus to care for us, he trusts us to make a home for him. Before he came, the Jews built a temple where they could worship God.

They believed that he lived in the Holy of Holies and the people would go there to offer sacrifices. Jesus told us that we no longer needed to do that because his death wiped out the need to sacrifice animals."

"Yeah, we just have to say sorry and mean it," said Sam.

Chris smiled, "That's right, but he also said that he would send his spirit to be with us always. Christians believe that his spirit lives inside us, joined with ours so that he can speak to us and help us whenever we need him to. I have to admit that I for one am really grateful, I need his help all the time!"

Sam opened his eyes wide, "Really? That's just...." He shook his head, lost for words. Sam was baffled, how could the God he had seen in the cloud during the exodus and heard as a rumble of thunder when they left the ark, live inside him?

"I know, incredible isn't it? But that's what he promised and whenever we need him we just have to ask."

Sam looked doubtful, this was just too crazy for words. But then, so was time travel! Chris could see that Sam was struggling so he grabbed a bible and turned to something near the back.

"Have you heard of Paul?" he asked.

"Er maybe, didn't he start out by killing the Christians? Wasn't it him who saw the light and ended up travelling all over the place to tell people about Jesus?"

"Yes, he did and during his travels, he wrote lots of letters that have been copied and included in the New Testament. Look at what he says in his letter to the church at Corinth – 'Don't you know that your body is the temple of the Holy Spirit, who lives in you and was given to you by God?' Then back here in his letter to the Romans, he says, 'God's Spirit joins himself to our spirits to declare that we are God's children.'"

Sam could see that Chris really believed this stuff, his eyes lit up whenever he read the bible and he sort of glowed with enthusiasm. He wished that he could believe the same as Chris did but he still wasn't quite convinced. How could the scary God who was cross enough to mix up everyone's language live inside Sam when some of the thoughts he'd been having about Ollie and Jack were practically unprintable!

"Look, why don't you just give him a go?" suggested Chris, "Next time you find yourself in a bit of bother, ask God to help. I think you'll be surprised."

Sam nodded, what did he have to lose? There was certainly no harm in trying. Besides, if God could take him as far back as the ark he could surely help him out with learning to love Jack. He wasn't so sure about Ollie though, Sam thought that may be one problem too many!

Walking home that night, Sam asked God to help him out with learning to love his enemies. Maybe I could be like the Samaritan and help Jack now he's on crutches he thought. He sighed, next week was going to be very interesting when he went back to school! Still, at least he had his trips to Bethlehem to look forward to!

Grinning to himself at the thought of more time travel adventures with Rachel, Matthew and Kate, Sam ran the rest of the way home excited at where the time stone would take him next.

GLOSSARY

Abba/Agya (Akan) – *Dad, daddy*

Altar – *Table of offerings to God*

Authority – *Power to give orders, expect obedience*

Covenant – *Promise or contract*

Delegation - *Group of representatives*

Didgeridoo – *Wind instrument (Australia)*

Ete-sen (Akan) – *Hello*

Extinct – *No longer exists*

Habitat – *Natural environment of a plant or animal*

Ima/Ena (Akan) – *Mum, mummy*

Instigate – C*ause something to happen*

Kundu – *Drum (Papua New Guinea)*

Levite – *Priests' assistant*

Missionary – *Someone sent to tell others about God*

Predator – *An animal that kills another for food*

Sacrifice – *Giving up something you value*

Samaritan – *From Samaria*

Shalom – *Peace*

Subside - *Lessen, go down, reduce*

Torah – *Jewish Bible*

Translate – *Change from one language to another*

Yahweh – *God*

BIBLE REFERENCES

If you would like to read about the events and places that Sam visited you will find them in the Christian bible. There are lots of different translations but one of the easiest to understand is the Good News Bible. If you don't have a Bible you can look them up on the internet.

Old Testament Stories

Noah – *Genesis ch 6 - 8*
Rainbow – *Genesis ch 9 vs 1 - 17*
Tower of Babel – *Genesis ch 11 vs 1 - 9*

New Testament Stories

Centurion's servant – *Luke ch 7 vs 1 - 10*
Good Samaritan – *Luke ch 10 vs 25 - 37*
Paul's vision – *Acts ch 9 vs 1 - 19*
Paul's words – *I Corinthians ch 6 vs 19*
Romans ch 8 vs 16

THE DODO

The dodo lived on the island of Mauritius, in the Indian Ocean. Not much is known about them as they became extinct in 1681. They were slightly bigger than a turkey and although unable to fly they may have been able to run quite fast. It is thought that dodos ate fruit, nuts and possibly crabs and shellfish which they would have broken into with their strong beaks.

Their beaks may also have been used to defend themselves although they didn't have many predators until men began to make their homes on the island. As forests were cut down to make space for human homes, the dodos had less space for theirs. Also, the pigs and macaque monkeys that were brought to the island by the people may have stolen their eggs for food. As it is likely they only produced one egg at a time, their numbers would have reduced quite quickly.

The extinction of the dodo shows how important it is to look after our world. Many animals are in danger of becoming extinct as their numbers are too low for them to survive. Some of those most endangered are elephants, rhinos and sea turtles, all of which are on the critical list of the World Wildlife Fund.

You can find out more about what they do and how you can help on their website but as always, do check with your responsible adult first!

God gave us this world to enjoy and he expects us to care for it. From the tiny bee which pollinates the plants that give us food and beautiful flowers, to the largest elephant – just because they are magnificent! He made them all and it is our job to look after them.

www.wwf.org.uk

BIBLE TRANSLATION

Wycliffe Bible Translators is a missionary organisation that sends people to countries around the world to learn new languages and write them down. They aim to translate the bible so that every person throughout the world can understand God's word.

There are at least 7,000 languages spoken or signed but only 700 of those languages have the complete bible translated into their language or a similar one they can understand. Translation work is being done in 2,700 languages but at least another 2,000 still need work to be started. 1.5 billion people do not have the full Bible in their language, which is more than all the people in the whole of Africa!

God gave us the Bible to teach us about his love and his purpose for mankind. He wants everyone to learn about him which is why the work of Wycliffe and other organisations like it are important.

If you would like to know more they have a great website with lots of fun activities that help you to learn about people and cultures around the world.

Don't forget to check with your responsible adult first though!

www.wycliffe.org/resources/kids/activities

ACKNOWLEDGEMENT

This is my favourite book so far! I really enjoyed writing about Sam's time on the ark. I learnt a lot about what life may have been like for Noah from the Verhalen Ark when it was docked in Ipswich.

When our children were young we spent time in Papua New Guinea and Australia where we served with Wycliffe Bible Translators. It is they who provided the information on languages around the world. I highly recommend the kids activity pages on their website.

Thanks as ever to all those who have prayed for and encouraged me. You are a blessing!

And of course, thanks to my best friend, Jesus, without whom Sam Parrow could not exist (and neither could I!)

ABOUT THE AUTHOR

Gill Parkes

Gill lives in Norfolk with her husband where she enjoys walks along the beach and exploring the countryside. She loves to spend time with her grandchildren, especially snuggling up to share a good book.

Jesus is her best friend and she hopes that by reading these stories you will get to know him too.

SAM PARROW'S TIME TRAVEL ADVENTURES

Sam travels through time to learn about God, how much he is loved and his own special place in God's world.

Sam Parrow And The Time Stone To Bethlehem

Sam Parrow Back In Time For Dinner

Sam Parrow And The Time Stone Secret

Sam Parrow Takes Time To Save A Dodo

Printed in Great Britain
by Amazon